Adalyn's Clare

Kari Dunn Buron

Illustrated by Lou Wisniewski

P.O. Box 23173
Shawnee Mission, Kansas 66283-0173
www.aapcpublishing.net

©2012 AAPC Publishing
P.O. Box 23173
Shawnee Mission, Kansas 66283-0173
www.aapcpublishing.net

Publisher's Cataloging-in-Publication

Buron, Kari Dunn.

Adalyn's Clare / Kari Dunn Buron ; illustrated by Lou Wisniewski. -- Shawnee Mission, Kan. : AAPC Publishing, c2012.

p. ; cm.

ISBN: 978-1-937473-22-8
LCCN: 2012943255
Audience: grades 3-6.
Summary: With the help of Clare, a specially trained labrador puppy, and the wise animals in the science lab, Adalyn learns to deal better with the ups and downs of everyday life at school.

1. Autistic children--Juvenile fiction. 2. Children with autism spectrum disorders--Juvenile fiction. 3. Dogs--Therapeutic use--Juvenile fiction. 4. Service dogs--Juvenile fiction. 5. Animals--Therapeutic use--Juvenile fiction. 6. [Autism--Fiction. 7. Dogs--Fiction. 8. Animals--Fiction.] I. Wisniewski, Lou. II. Title.

PZ7.B93758 A33 2012
[E]--dc23 1208

This book is designed in Palatino and Helvetica Neue.

Printed in the United States of America.

In memory of June Dunn

and

In honor of June Wisniewski

CONTENTS

Chapter One: Adalyn

Sometimes a pop-up tent is like a hug, giving just enough security and comfort to make life bearable again. This was Adalyn's thought as she rubbed her legs and tried to slow down her breathing. Fifteen minutes earlier she had been in her classroom, about to scream at someone or throw something.

Actually, the day had started out pretty good. Adalyn had done her homework and was feeling almost excited about showing her paper to her teacher, Miss Thomas. But when she got to her classroom, she noticed that Miss Thomas wasn't in the room. Instead, there, at the front of the room, was Mr. Hirtle, the student teacher.

Adalyn did not want to turn her paper into Mr. Hirtle; she wanted to turn it in to her **real** teacher, Miss Thomas. Why did teachers have student teachers anyway? Student teachers never knew about special programs. Student teachers always wanted to be the boss of everyone. Mr. Hirtle used an angry-sounding voice whenever Adalyn asked to go to her pop-up tent, even though it was on her official plan! The last time Adalyn had needed a break, Mr. Hirtle said something out loud in front of all the other kids about how she should be able to handle things better; about how she was nine years old, and how nine-year-olds weren't supposed to have tantrums. That's for two-year-olds.

The thought of Miss Thomas being absent and Mr. Hirtle being in charge gave Adalyn an instant stomachache. She started breathing too fast and thinking of ways to strip Mr. Hirtle of his student teaching status. To avoid having a "two-year-old tantrum," or possibly worse, Adalyn grabbed the hall pass and quickly left the room.

Mrs. Kelly was a special teacher who helped students who had problems at school. Her room was a quiet place for kids to go and relax and learn about how to handle the stuff that was really hard to handle.

Mrs. Kelly called the pop-up tent Adalyn's safe place; the place she could go to when life, and school, and student teachers made her feel crazy. The tent was a Spitfire Solo; it felt like a sanctuary, with its totally secure zipper door and full-coverage fly and black-out window coverings. It was a place to rethink the bad thoughts and quiet her body. It was a place where she could take her brain on a much-needed time-out journey, far away from people, rules, and talk about "age-appropriate behavior."

Adalyn's mother had given her a globe of the world to keep in the tent. When she was having a particularly bad day, Adalyn would spin the globe, close her eyes, and then place her finger on the globe to stop it. Whatever country her finger was touching would be her destination, and she would begin to repeat all of the facts she knew about that place.

She particularly liked to think about the animals that lived in whatever country she pointed to. Adalyn loved animals more than just about anything else in the world. She loved domesticated animals like dogs, cats, white rats, and hamsters; she loved wild animals like tigers, bears, lions, and timber wolves. Animals just seemed easier than people.

Sitting safely in her tent, Adalyn spun the globe. Her finger landed on Tanzania, Africa. "Country in Eastern Africa, bordering the Indian Ocean," she started saying out loud. "The official language is Swahili; it is the home of the highest mountain in Africa, Mount Kilimanjaro." Amazingly, Adalyn was feeling better already.

"'Tingatinga' is a folk art style of painting started in Tanzania." She repeated the word "Tingatinga" – she often repeated words that felt fun in her mouth. "Home of the western white-bearded wildebeest," she continued, and then thought about how a white-bearded wildebeest might have a tantrum if it was blocked from making its migratory journey across the Serengeti.

Chapter Two: Clare

As Adalyn drifted further and further into her Tanzanian adventure, she sensed something approaching. Was it a wildebeest? Was it the wicked Mr. Hirtle?

Adalyn let out a breath of air as she slowly opened her eyes and eased her head toward the full-coverage fly. She gazed out through the specially designed peek hole in the black-out window. There, between Mrs. Kelly's foot and the pop-up tent's totally secure zipper door, stood the cutest little labrador retriever puppy Adalyn had ever seen.

"Oh my jeepers sakes!" exclaimed an excited Adalyn. "Who is that?" As she talked, she quickly unzipped the door to get a better look.

"This is my new puppy," said Mrs. Kelly. "She will be working here at school."

"What's her name?" asked Adalyn, as she inched her way closer to the yellow puppy.

"I haven't named her yet. I was hoping someone here might have a good idea for a name," said Mrs. Kelly.

"What about Clare?" suggested Adalyn. "My mother is from Meteghan, Nova Scotia, on the Acadian coast, in a region known as Clare. Clare is an almost perfect name for a girl, and she is a girl, right?"

Mrs. Kelly laughed, delighted by Adalyn's enthusiasm. She rarely saw Adalyn excited, or even happy. School was a hard place for a girl like Adalyn. More than anything, Mrs. Kelly wanted to make life a little easier for her. She was hoping to help Adalyn find a friend her own age; someone she could trust; someone who would appreciate Adalyn's amazing talents; someone Adalyn could relax with.

"Yes, she is a girl, and I think Clare is a perfect name," replied Mrs. Kelly.

Adalyn looked over at Clare, her face softening. Then she reached out, and Clare walked right into her arms. Adalyn felt a burst of happiness and quietly said, "Snagly." This was one of her very favorite words to say, and one of Adalyn's safe words; the word she would say when her anxieties and worries were less intense, and she was no longer feeling like all of humanity was out to get her.

Mrs. Kelly could tell that Adalyn was very interested in Clare, so she brought out a list of things that needed to be done with the new puppy every day:

1. Take her for a walk: 3 times a day (with poop bags)
2. Feed her: 1 time a day (around noon)

3. Play ball with her: 1 time a day before her lunch
4. Help her meet people: Every day by walking her through the hallways, taking her to class, and letting her hang out in the library.

Mrs. Kelly sat down with Adalyn and asked her if she would like to take some responsibility for Clare while she was at school. "You don't have to do everything if you don't want to, and every morning you can let me know if you want to do one thing, or two things, or all four things."

Adalyn could hardly believe her own ears. Besides Mr. Spencer's science room, this might be the best thing that had ever happened to her in her whole school life! "I want to do all four things," she yelled. "I can take her on a walk right now. She probably doesn't know much about the playground yet, and I know where all the good spots are."

"Great," said Mrs. Kelly. "Here are some special poop bags. I know how you kind of hate the feel of squishy things, so I found these really thick bags that are made so your hand doesn't have to get too close to the poop."

Adalyn chuckled a bit, but then winced as she thought about touching poop. Then she laughed out loud because Mrs. Kelly had said the word "poop." She put Clare's leash on her and walked her out to the big yard at the south end of the school.

Chapter 3: Deer Poop

Typically, Adalyn did not even like going outside for recess. The kids were too loud; they played too rough and talked too fast. She often thought that recess might be easier if only she had a friend, and she actually thought she would have a friend by now. Every year she silently wished for a friend, but every year ended the same, friendless.

It was only 10:15 in the morning, and there were no other kids out at recess yet. Adalyn and Clare had the whole place to themselves. The first place she took Clare was to the slide. Adalyn loved the slide. It was practically impossible to use the slide at recess, because there was always a line of kids waiting to go down. Adalyn did not like lines; she didn't like waiting, and often wondered why she couldn't just have all the turns. It didn't make sense; lines just made life miserable!

Without anyone else around for a change, Adalyn dropped Clare's leash and ran to the slide. She went up the ladder and down the slide four times in a row. It felt like heaven! This was the only way to really enjoy a slide.

As Adalyn circled around for turn number five, Clare followed her right up the stairs and down the slide! Adalyn thought this was pretty impressive. Clare was only three months old, and she could already watch and copy. Adalyn felt a wave of admiration flowing through her. She smiled at Clare, and Clare seemed to smile back.

Then Adalyn walked Clare to the patch of pine trees near the southeast corner of the school property. She loved the smell of pine trees and often left the playground to walk out among the trees and just smell and smell and smell. Even on a cold, snowy day in Minnesota, the pine tress smelled delicious.

Adalyn was lost in thought when she noticed that Clare was pulling on her leash. As she glanced over at the puppy, she was mortified to see her gobbling up a large pile of deer poop! Adalyn almost threw up.

"Clare, no!" she yelled. "Don't eat the deer poop!"

Clare looked up, deer poop still stuck to her nose, and she thought:

"I am only a three-month-old puppy. I don't really know the ways of the world yet, particularly when it comes to food. My mother taught me that the main rule of eating was to do it. Mother was raised in a hunting camp up north on Lake of the Woods, and she would spend hours telling my brothers and me stories about living in the woods. One thing she mentioned often was the joy of eating all kinds of droppings from all kinds of forest animals, and if not eating it, rolling in it!"

"We are going in now." Adalyn said briskly, and with that, she pulled on the leash and coaxed Clare back to the school building.

"This is unacceptable!" Adalyn shouted to nobody in particular. "This is totally and completely unacceptable!"

Chapter Four: The Sign

Adalyn rushed into Mrs. Kelly's room with little Clare dragging behind. Even though Mrs. Kelly was busy reading a story to two other students, Adalyn walked right up to the group.

"Clare ate deer poop!" she announced in a loud voice.

Mrs. Kelly silently held up one finger. This was one of their secret signs, and it usually meant that Adalyn had just interrupted somebody, and should stop talking. Adalyn backed away from the group as she felt her nerves mounting. First, Clare ate disgusting deer poop, and now she would have to wait forever until Mrs. Kelly was finished with her stupid story before she could tell her what had happened!

Adalyn felt a growl in her stomach and a tight feeling in her throat. Her mother called these "worries," and right now Adalyn was trying really hard not to let her worries get too big. She walked around the room three times, took three slow, deep breaths, and then focused on staying silent. Adalyn was learning about keeping her words inside her head when her worries got big. She then sat down on the floor, pulled her knees to her chest, and closed her eyes.

Just then, Clare crept up close and gently put her chin on Adalyn's foot. They waited there together, silently and relaxed, as Adalyn's nerves started to get smaller.

Mrs. Kelly finished her story, and walked over to Adalyn and Clare. Long ago, she had figured out that it was sometimes best to give Adalyn time to calm down before talking to her. Adalyn was one of those kids who got really upset really fast and sometimes needed help putting things into perspective. She was a very sweet girl, but her nervousness could get her into trouble if she wasn't careful, and Mrs. Kelly was helping her sort out the difficult moments.

Adalyn looked up when she sensed Mrs. Kelly near. "Clare ate deer poop, and I thought I was going to throw up," she said.

Mrs. Kelly smiled. "Clare is a dog. Not only is she a dog, but she is a labrador retriever, and labs have the dubious reputation of trying to eat anything that will fit in their mouths, whether we think it is tasty or not," she explained.

At that, Mrs. Kelly started to laugh, which also made Adalyn laugh. Laughing is a really good way to relax.

"I have an idea," said Adalyn. "I will make a sign to remind Clare not to eat deer poop."

Adalyn had several signs of her own posted around Mrs. Kelly's resource room, as well as in her desk back in Miss Thomas' room. Her signs reminded her to do things, like take deep breaths, take a drink of water, and say thank you. Some of the signs in Miss Thomas' room were for all the kids, like the red alert sign she posted when there was homework and the one near her desk that said "Put Homework Here."

Mrs. Kelly thought the sign idea was great. In fact, she thought it was such a good idea that she told Susan about it and asked her if she wanted to help make the sign.

Susan was another kid who sometimes came down to Mrs. Kelly's room. Adalyn didn't really like working with other kids, but Susan seemed to think the idea was "absolutely brilliant!" so Adalyn took another deep breath and made a smiling face to show Susan that she was in a friendly mood.

"I cracked up laughing when I heard that the puppy ate deer poop," said Susan. "Making a sign will be absolutely, over-the-top hysterical!"

Adalyn remained quiet, not really sure what to say. She wondered how anyone could possibly think that eating deer poop was funny. Did Susan mean making a sign would be funny as in ironical, or "funny ha-ha"? By the time Adalyn had thought this through, Susan was already at the other end of the room talking to someone else.

Adalyn decided on a big universal "no" sign laid over a picture illustrating what looked like a pile of round biscuits. She thought Clare might understand the message if she drew a picture. After completing the sign, she shyly crossed the room and showed it to Susan, who thought it was absolutely "fantastical."

Chapter Five: The Science Room

Three weeks later, Mrs. Kelly felt that Clare was ready to travel with Adalyn to some of the other rooms in the school. She put together a little "travel bag" for Clare, with a collapsible pouch for water and a small rolled-up mat to use as a bed. The day before, she and Adalyn had agreed to start with the science room and see how things went.

Adalyn arrived at Mrs. Kelly's room, excited at the prospect of introducing Clare to Mr. Spencer. Mr. Spencer was her very favorite teacher. Actually, he was one of her very favorite people in the whole world. Her mother called Mr. Spencer an "appreciator," which she explained was someone who liked a lot of things and who noticed the special things about both animals and people. Adalyn could sense that most people thought she was different and strange, but Mr. Spencer thought she was smart and clever.

When Adalyn and Clare arrived at the science room, they were greeted by Mr. Spencer, who was visiting with the school principal, Mr. Peterson.

"Adalyn, I have some great news," said Mr. Peterson when he saw her enter the room. "Your zoology project made it past the preliminary judges and is going to the state fair!"

Adalyn got so excited at this news that she totally forgot about Clare. "I just knew that a project involving the paternal role of the New Zealand kiwi would be sure to catch their collective eyes," she said enthusiastically.

Mr. Peterson smiled and thought, "What a strange child this Adalyn is." On one hand, she often had problems that were serious enough to be called to his attention; on the other hand, she had just written an amazing science paper worthy of a college student.

Mr. Spencer smiled and thought, "What a brilliant child!" He was feeling very proud of Adalyn, and extra happy that Mr. Peterson was here to see her in such a positive light.

"We will need to clean up parts of your introduction and the wording of your main idea, but I think you have a good chance at the grand prize," said Mr. Spencer.

As the three of them stood there, beaming about Adalyn's success, Clare's little otter-like tail started to pound against the floor.

"Oh my," said Mr. Peterson looking down at Clare, "and who is this?"

"This is Clare. I named her Clare after my mother's birthplace in Nova Scotia. Mrs. Kelly has assigned her to me for safe keeping!" announced Adalyn proudly.

"Oh yes," said Mr. Peterson. "I think I have heard about this puppy. So, do you think she will be good at making friends?"

"She is a canine, and as such is prone to social behavior," offered Adalyn. "She is only four months old, but she's a fast learner."

Mr. Peterson smiled and gave Clare a welcome pat. He then excused himself, reminding Mr. Spencer that they both needed to be at a meeting in his office in ten minutes.

Mr. Spencer smiled at Adalyn and then at Clare. "I think she is exquisite. I'm sure she will want to meet the less human inhabitants of our science room. Why don't you do the honors before you go to lunch?"

With that, Adalyn walked Clare to the far end of the science room to introduce her to her most favorite friends in the whole wide world. As Clare approached the animal cages, she could sense the calm in Adalyn.

"This is Pixie," said Adalyn, as she picked up a beautiful brown ferret. She is one of my best friends, and always the first one to greet me when I enter the room."

Clare gave Pixie a sniff, and Pixie gave Clare a sniff in return. Clare thought that Pixie was exceptionally pretty but that she had a very curious aroma. After smelling Clare, Pixie silently identified mud, lake water, Kibble®, and tennis balls.

"And over here, we have Orin," said Adalyn. "He is from the southern part of Essex, England, and is able to negotiate fifty-eight different mazes with no problem."

Clare looked across the room where Adalyn was holding up a big white rat. Her first thought was how much fun it would be to chase Orin, but then she remembered that this was Adalyn's friend and that she needed to think and act in a friendly way.

Next, Clare met Julia, a motmot bird from Trinidad and Tobago; Nancy, the hairless rat; Carter, a very large snapping turtle from the north shore of Minnesota; and finally, Alejandro, a three-legged guinea pig from South America.

After Adalyn had introduced all of the animals to Clare, she took out the traveling kit Mrs. Kelly had given her. She filled the portable bowl with water and laid the travel mat near Mr. Spencer's desk.

It was time for her to go to lunch, so she gave Clare a scratch behind the ears and told her to wait in the science room until she came back. She hung Clare's leash on a chair and assured her that after lunch, they would go for a walk.

As Clare watched Adalyn leave, she stretched out her legs and curled up on the soft new mat. She closed her eyes and was almost asleep, when she heard a high-pitched, almost whiney-sounding voice.

"You have your work cut out for you, mate," said the unfamiliar voice.

Chapter Six: Animal Consultants

Claire raised her head and caught sight of Orin, the rat, perched on the top of his cage, just as all the other animals in the room started to talk.

"She has no idea."

"Poor little puppy."

"She probably hasn't met Mrs. Waddle yet."

"She'll have to watch her back."

"She'll have to think on her feet."

All of a sudden, Clare cried out, "Stop!"

"Yes. If we speak one at a time, it is easier for everyone to be heard," added Orin. "I will start."

Orin approached Clare slowly and said, "Please excuse our excitement. It is just that we all love Adalyn. She is interested in us, she cares about us, and she protects us from careless, less informed humans."

Nancy scurried up to join Orin and continued, "Adalyn comes to the science room to hide from the other humans. The young humans make fun of her because she is different."

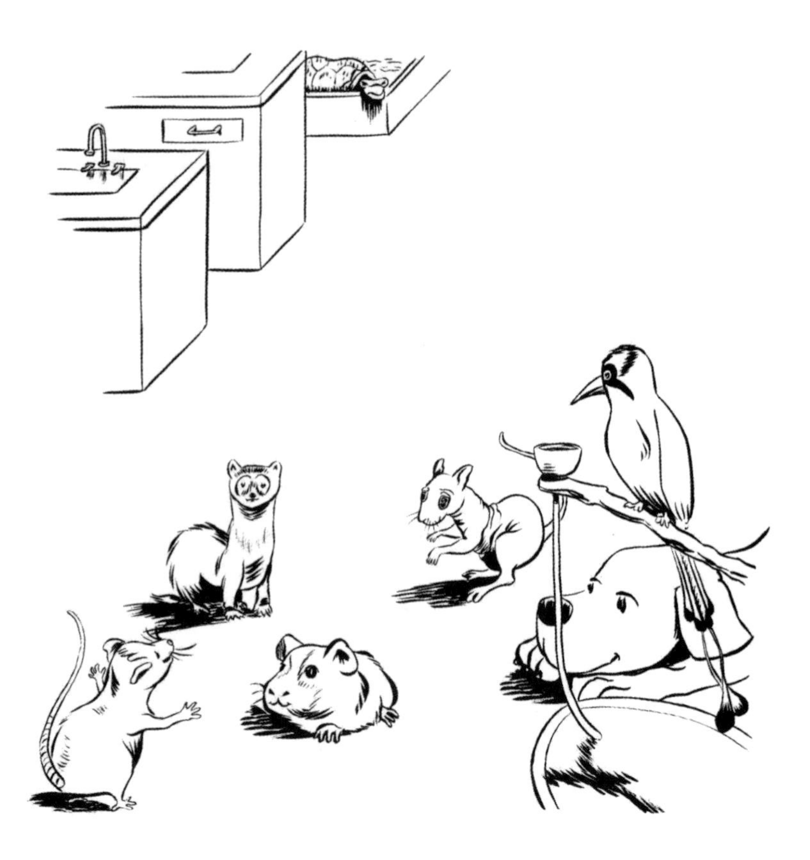

In a deep South American accent, Alejandro added, "I know a thing or two about being different, and Adalyn is most certainly different."

Next it was Carter's turn. He spoke up from his large pen across the room, "I could snap off a human toe in a single second!"

"What?" asked Clare.

"Don't mind Carter," Orin reassured her. "Just smile and nod."

Clare was getting very confused … and more than a little nervous. What exactly was her job? Why did everyone here think it was going to be hard?

As if reading her mind, Pixie said gently, "Don't fret too badly, miss puppy. I think you are perfect for the job. You are very cute to look at and soft to the touch. Adalyn needs soft things, and the other humans like cute things. Yes, you are decidedly a good choice."

Miss Julia, who was new to the science room herself, thought that all this talk was probably too much, too fast for the puppy. So she said, "Stop for a minute. This is too much 'preshah.' Let's all relax and tell little Miss Clare a bit about ourselves."

There were nods all around and sounds of approval, everyone wondering why they had not thought of this first. Clare was relieved no longer to be the focus of attention. She looked at Julia with grateful eyes.

Since it was her idea, Julia started. She told Clare that she was born on the Caribbean island of Tobago, in the village of Speyside. She had been very happy in Tobago before her capture, but said she had not had a single happy day since. After her traumatic abduction, she came to live in the Exotic Bird Sanctuary just outside of St. Paul, Minnesota. Then, as if that wasn't enough bad luck for one lifetime, the director of the sanctuary put a rather aggressive magnificent frigate bird in her area, who immediately started to steal everyone's food!

Julia was vexed! Being a proponent of fair play, she decided to fight back. But the magnificent frigate bird, who was five times bigger than Julia, had other ideas. In the end, Julia was injured so seriously that the sanctuary's director decided to call his friend, Mr. Spencer, and ask if he would provide a safe place for Julia to mend.

Clare thought Julia was the most exotic bird in the world, with a story of trauma and adventure that she could barely imagine. She also absolutely loved Julia's smooth, rhythmic way of speaking.

Nancy spoke up next. She said that she was originally from Oklahoma City, where she had been born in a lab at the university. She was a "lifer," she added. Officially, she was a "Cavia Porcellus," Nancy explained, which is a person or thing used as a subject of research. She was not one to complain and was actually quite proud of the studies she had participated in. As a hairless rat, she knew she would never be particularly appealing as a pet, and being born in a lab, she lacked the skills necessary to live in the wild. It was her dream, as it was with most "lifers," to one day be a part of some wonderful cure, she confessed.

As Orin got ready to tell his story, the door to the science room opened, and in walked Adalyn and Mr. Spencer. Clare knew that it was time for a walk, and maybe some tennis ball fetching. Even though these were two of her top favorite things, she found herself hoping she could return to the science room soon to learn more about her interesting new friends.

Chapter Seven: The Library

The next day, Mrs. Kelly asked Adalyn to take Clare with her to the library, another favorite spot for Adalyn, and one where there would be other children. Her hope was that if Adalyn had Clare with her, the other children would want to be with her, too.

Clare was exceptionally friendly, and the other children around the school were already curious about her as the rumor had spread about Mrs. Kelly's dog. Just the other day, two girls from another fourth-grade room had come down to the resource room and asked if they could play with Clare. Mrs. Kelly had explained that Clare was a working dog and that she would be working with Adalyn to help her feel more comfortable with other kids.

The two girls listened closely to Mrs. Kelly. They could not imagine being nervous around other kids. They could understand being nervous around adults, or being nervous about taking a test, but who ever heard of being nervous around other kids?

Adalyn could hardly wait to get to the library, so she and Clare walked quickly, trying hard not to run in the hallway. Adalyn was sure that Miss Dudley would love Clare. Miss Dudley was the librarian, and she had like a zillion pets of her own. She had four cats and two dogs at home. Besides, she had twenty-eight fish in the library fish tank, an ant colony, and three teddy bear hamsters. She clearly loved animals, and she would love Clare.

"Good morning, Miss Dudley," Adalyn said as she entered the library. "This is Clare, who was aptly named after the area of Nova Scotia my mother hales from. Mrs. Kelly allowed me to name her, and she is my responsibility here at school. I am helping Clare get familiar with the school building."

"Wow," replied Miss Dudley with a big smile. "Welcome to our very dog-friendly library, Miss Clare!"

Clare bounced right up to Miss Dudley and licked her fingers. "What a cute puppy. She must smell my dogs and cats. She seems to like me."

"Mrs. Kelly said that Clare likes everybody," replied Adalyn. "Not to take away from your excitement, but I think it is her job to like people."

"Well, I think that so far, she is doing a very good job!" exclaimed Miss Dudley. "By the way, today I would like you to re-shelve the returned books."

Adalyn had an official job in the library, but she was also assigned to Miss Dudley the same way she was assigned to Mr. Spencer. They were called "mentors." Mrs. Kelly had picked them because they had naturally good feelings for Adalyn, and Adalyn needed more people to have good feelings about her.

Adalyn started organizing her book cart just as Mrs. Waddle's fourth-grade class came into the library. Adalyn could feel herself tense up just a bit because Mrs. Waddle sometimes yelled at her students, and that always made her nervous.

When Adalyn's mother had met with Mrs. Kelly last year to talk about Adalyn moving on to fourth grade, Adalyn had overheard Mrs. Kelly say that Miss Thomas would be the best choice for teacher.

Adalyn knew she was smart. She was a regular fourth grader, who did regular fourth-grade work, in a regular fourth-grade classroom. But Adalyn also knew she needed a little support. She needed someone like Mrs. Kelly to help her navigate the really hard parts of school. She needed her pop-up tent and a place to go when her worries got too big. She also needed someone to do tricky things, like picking the right teacher.

ART

Chapter Eight: Adalyn's Particularly Bad Moment

Clare stayed with Adalyn while she organized the books on her cart, but she soon found herself distracted and wandered into Miss Dudley's office to investigate a particularly interesting smell. Meanwhile, Adalyn pushed the cart out to the main area of the library, and among the fourth-graders from Mrs. Waddle's room.

As Adalyn turned down the Westerns aisle, she was startled to see Richard Riker, a fourth grader with a reputation for being nasty and mean, looking at her with an intense stare.

"Do you have any good Westerns on that cart?" Richard asked.

"You are not allowed to take a book off this cart," Adalyn replied promptly. "The books must be re-shelved first. Then you can take a book off the shelf and take it up to Miss Dudley's desk for check out."

"Who are you anyway?" asked Richard. "Miss nerd librarian? Miss 'I'm too afraid to get in trouble'? Miss 'I can't break any rules or I'll be doomed'?" And just then, without any regard for protocol or consequences, Richard Riker took a book off the cart!

"No!" screamed Adalyn. "You can't! You mustn't!" She was visibly upset, and that only seemed to make Richard meaner.

"Oh no," he said sarcastically. "The world will end! Look out, someone took a stupid book off of the stupid cart, and now the pretend librarian is gonna get in big trouble."

Adalyn was desperate. Her throat started to ache, and her legs felt weak. She wanted to hit Richard Riker in his big, ugly, nasty mouth!

Miss Dudley and Clare were in the office, and Mrs. Waddle was across the room. Her nerves were racing too fast, and she was spinning out of control! She pulled together every bit of self-control she had and ran out of the library, towards Mrs. Kelly's room and the safety of the pop-up tent.

But when Adalyn arrived at the resource room, the door was locked! "Nooo!" she screamed. There was a sign on the door. Adalyn's eyes were blurry, but she managed to read what the sign said: "At a meeting, back soon."

"NOOOOOO!" Adalyn screamed, even louder. Classroom doors all around started opening, and teachers were coming out into the hallway. Mrs. Waddle's class was there. Kids were staring! Richard Riker was laughing! Adalyn's head felt like it was going to explode, and she thought, "**I'm going to kill Richard Riker!**" But she didn't just think it. She ***screamed*** it out loud.

About a hundred more kids were staring at her, and some unfamiliar teachers were walking towards her. She turned and started running. She ran outside, and she kept on running.

She ran through the neighborhood until she had run eight blocks ... all the way home. She ran into her house, right past her mother, and upstairs to her bedroom. She immediately got into her bed and pulled the covers over her head, desperately wishing she could be transported to another world; another universe where rules were clear, where people were logical, and where there was most definitely no horrible Richard Riker!

Chapter Nine: The Meeting

There are many hard things about being a fourth grader, but Adalyn thought there wasn't anything harder than this.

She looked around the big table in the principal's room ... at her mother and father, Mrs. Kelly, Mr. Spencer, Mr. Peterson, Miss Dudley, the wicked Mr. Hirtle, and the icky Mrs. Waddle. She was doomed for sure.

In the corner of the room lay Clare, watching, listening, and feeling as guilty as any four-month-old puppy could possibly feel. She had dropped the ball! Abandoned her charge! Deserted the ship! She needed to listen closely to the adult humans. She needed to figure out what she, just a little yellow dog, could do to help.

"I'm open to any and all suggestions," Mr. Peterson was saying. "The district's position is clear. Threatening the life of another person results in suspension from school."

"With all due respect, Mr. Peterson, aren't we over-interpreting what happened here?" asked

Adalyn's father. "Addie is a good girl, a little hot-headed perhaps, but she would never hurt another being, human or otherwise."

"I agree," said Mrs. Kelly. "Adalyn was clearly being teased by Richard, and unfortunately no adult was near enough to recognize it and end it before it got out of control."

"I disagree," said Mrs. Waddle. "Adalyn made a clear and direct threat. I heard it, as did about one hundred other people. Richard made no similar threat. She needs to learn a lesson. I vote for suspension!"

"I disagree," said Mr. Spencer. "Adalyn is a very sensitive child. She is particularly vulnerable to the taunts of others. When someone attacks her, she responds on a very basic level. She gets angry, but she is not violent."

Adalyn was beginning to feel invisible. She was right here, and they were all talking about her as if she wasn't there. It felt like she was on trial. Maybe that was it – she was on trial, and everyone was either defending her or prosecuting her. If found guilty, she would be "suspended," but Adalyn wasn't sure exactly what that meant, or how that would help her with her worries.

Sensing Adalyn's discomfort, Clare walked to her side and put her smooth snout on Adalyn's lap. She raised her big sad puppy eyes toward Adalyn. Direct looks like these were sometimes hard for Adalyn, but it was the best way for Clare to show her support.

Adalyn noticed Clare's look, and felt her support. She closed her eyes and whispered, "Snagly." She had no choice but to wait silently for her fate to be decided.

After almost an hour, it was done. Although Mr. Peterson admitted that Mrs. Kelly had some good points in defense of Adalyn, he was bound to the rules of the school district, he said. Adalyn had clearly threatened Richard. There were at least a dozen witnesses, and Richard was claiming to be emotionally distraught, fearful for his very life. Adalyn would be suspended from school for one week!

Clare was devastated as she watched Adalyn walk out of the building with her parents. She would not see her friend for a whole week. "Why?" she thought. Once again, she began to reflect on what her own mother had told her before she left the farm to live with Mrs. Kelly. She remembered her telling Clare that she was surely going to make a lot of mistakes; she had said that making mistakes was what being a puppy was all about.

"A good human won't punish you," her mother had said. "Instead, she will guide you away from the mistake and then let you know when you are being a good dog."

Chapter Ten: Animal Sense

"Outrageous!" declared Nancy. "This is not justice; this is incompetence. The research supports me on this one. Suspension is no more than punishment, and punishment does not serve to teach anything!"

"We can go on and on about how we feel, or how things should be," said Orin, "or we can think about how to help Clare. She's the only one around here who is in a position to help Adalyn. She's the one who might actually make a difference."

"Well, I for one would like to know where little Miss Clare was when our Adalyn was being tormented by that horrible Richard Riker?" exclaimed Alejandro. "Can she even be trusted?"

"Alejandro, you need to let – it – go," said Julia, in her laid-back manner. "The poor child made a mistake; she's only a baby. Bullies are hard even for grown animals to understand. We can understand hurting for food; or hurting for shelter; and certainly hurting to protect our babies; but hurting for fun makes no good sense."

"I could snap off a bully's nose in a single second!" offered Carter.

"Let's focus," said Orin, as Clare watched him with admiration.

Orin had been born in the sewers of Essex, England. He considered himself a "Southender," which is what many of the rats from the southeast part of England called themselves. When he was still quite young, he had made his way into a human house and created a very comfortable bed inside an old couch.

One day in the spring, Orin and his couch were set out on the street. At first he was thrilled to have both the fresh air and a soft bed in the same place, but soon he and his bed were picked up by some humans and taken far away to another town. The town turned out to be Cambridge, home to the famous Cambridge University. A university student had picked up Orin's couch and was using it in what Orin referred to as a "hall of residence."

After a year, when the stuffing was almost completely beaten out of the couch, Orin decided to move on. He made his way to the science building where things were unusually clean, and where he was quickly spotted by a human, who immediately set out a plate of Brie for him. But just as Orin was about to dine on the delicious French cheese, another human grabbed the dish away.

"Don't poison it," the second human said. "I need all the rats I can get! Let's catch it alive."

Although Orin had just heard this plan, he was still unable to resist another go at the Brie. The new cheese was placed inside a cage, and that was how he became a lab rat at Cambridge University.

Orin had learned a lot during his tenure at Cambridge, and the animals trusted his good sense. And it was with good sense that he began to discuss a plan to help Clare help Adalyn.

"It is clear to me that Adalyn needs a pack," started Orin. "If I had traveled with a pack back in the good old days, I might still be a free rat."

"I agree," said Pixie. "Adalyn needs a pack for protection, or as ferrets would say, a business."

"And a pack could bring her such joy," added Julia, thinking about how happy she would be if she had even one other motmot to play with.

Clare listened with great interest. "I had some litter mates that were like a pack," she said. "I loved all my litter mates, but there were two who loved tennis balls just as much as I did. They were my favorite pack friends."

"Excellent thinking," offered Nancy. "Adalyn loves almost everything about science. There are bound to be other human pups in this school who love science, too."

Chapter Eleven: In Search of a Pack

Mrs. Kelly decided to let Clare spend the week in the science room. She knew that Adalyn would be spending much of her time there, and she wanted Clare to become relaxed and comfortable with the various animals, noises, and smells in the room.

Clare could hardly believe her luck, and for the next few days she followed Mr. Spencer. He taught science to all of the fourth, fifth, and sixth graders, which totaled approximately 128 students. While Mr. Spencer was teaching, Clare watched the children. She was looking for signs of love and enthusiasm. Pixie had told her about enthusiasm, and even demonstrated what she called her Weasel War Dance, a very enthusiastic routine that ferrets do when they are particularly excited.

So far, Clare had not noticed anything quite as dramatic as the Weasel War Dance, but she did notice two students who appeared to be paying extra attention, looking more often at the teacher and answering more questions. One student was called Henry, and he was a fourth grader just like Adalyn. The other student was called Vicente; he was a sixth grader.

Mr. Spencer was talking about geography this month, and both Henry and Vicente seemed very interested in things like continents, mountains, and glaciers. Clare remembered watching Adalyn with her globe in the pop-up tent and began to feel hopeful that she might have found the beginning of a suitable pack for her.

Two days earlier, Clare had asked Julia if she had any ideas about creating a pack. "How can I make it happen?" she had asked.

Julia had given this a lot of thought, and was quite pleased that Clare chose to ask her for advice. She told Clare that she had four really good friends back in Tobago, another motmot bird name Gareth, two parrots named James and Wilfred, and a rainbow lorikeet named Rebecca. She first met Gareth because he lived in the same tree as she did. Gareth knew James and Wilfred from his trips to the rainforest, and Wilfred had met Rebecca "liming" on the fishing docks of Speyside. She knew one, who knew another, who knew another, and soon they all knew each other!

"I believe that is how it works," said Julia. "Since you are already Adalyn's friend, it seems the next step is for you to make friends with Henry and Vicente!"

On Friday of the week without Adalyn, Clare went to the library to visit Miss Dudley. While there, she noticed a girl human who came to the library three times in that one day, which was odd indeed. Every time she came in, she sat by herself. On the girl's third visit, Clare watched her walk in by herself, and sit by herself.

"I wonder," thought Clare, "if this is another human child in need of a pack?"

Clare walked slowly over to the table, so as not to startle the child. She sat about two feet from the table, and started to send the girl "look at me" thoughts. This was a technique Clare used with Mrs. Kelly and her family when she wanted them to wake up and feed her breakfast.

Only one minute into the look, the girl turned and noticed Clare. Clare's happy otter-like tail started wagging to let the girl know that she was in a friendly mood.

"Oh my. Where did you come from?" said the girl as she reached out and scratched Clare behind her ears.

"This is a girl who knows her dogs," thought Clare. Then she glanced over and noticed a picture of stars on the open page of the girl's book.

"Stars," thought Clare. "I will have to ask Orin and Nancy, but I am pretty sure stars are a part of science!"

Clare left the library that day feeling like she could do the Weasel War Dance! She was going to give Adalyn the best present ever. She would find her a pack.

Chapter Twelve: Time Served

Adalyn was desperate to find her science paper. She crept through the darkened hallway towards Mrs. Kelly's room. The door was not only locked, but pad-locked, with streams of crime scene tape blocking any access.

"The library!" she thought. "I might have left it in the library."

The school was dark and abandoned, and the halls seemed endless. She could see the library but couldn't seem to reach it. Suddenly she heard a sound! Someone was walking in the hallway! Adalyn looked around, terrified, searching for a place to hide. She found a stairway, and quickly ducked into the shadows.

Within seconds, the wicked Mr. Hirtle came around the corner and bellowed, "I know you're in here, you little two-year-old fourth grader. It is only a matter of time before I track you down!"

Adalyn shivered uncontrollably and willed herself invisible.

"You can't escape your destiny!" bellowed Mr. Hirtle. "I will find you, and when I do you, I will pin back your ears, butter your head, and **swallow you whole**!"

Just then Mr. Hirtle's head whipped around the stairway corner. Adalyn closed her eyes and screamed! She screamed, and screamed, and screamed until she heard a gentle voice.

"Addie, you are having another nightmare, her mother whispered. "Shhhhh … it's OK, honey. I'm right here."

Adalyn had been having nightmares every night since that horrible meeting at school. She had always worried that the other children at school didn't like her, and now she was worried that the teachers didn't like her either. Sure, Mrs. Kelly had defended her, and Mr. Spencer seemed to give her the benefit of the doubt, but what must they be thinking about her? Now that she had been found guilty by the entire school board! These thoughts made Adalyn's head hurt, and they had made their way into her dreams.

Adalyn was mortified, embarrassed, and more worried than ever. What would she say to Miss Thomas? How could she face Miss Dudley? Did everyone think she was a criminal? Would everyone be afraid of her from now on?

As the week of her suspension was coming to an end and it was time for Adalyn to return to school, she begged her parents to let her take coursework online, or maybe start fresh at a different school – anything but going back to her old school. When these ideas were rejected, she started to fantasize about having a burst appendix or inflamed tonsils and a temperature of 103.

Monday morning brought even more worries and tears; Adalyn was sure it was going to be the worst day of her whole school life. She made a few more desperate attempts to convince her mother that she would die if she had to go back to school, but her mother just hugged her, smoothed her hair, and told her things would be OK. After breakfast, she helped Adalyn gather her homework papers, made her a lunch with an extra cookie, and then together they walked to the car.

As she rode the final blocks to school, Adalyn practiced her deep breathing; she closed her eyes and tried to visualize the animals she might find in Brazil. She got out of the car still thinking about maned wolves, crab-eating foxes, and capuchin monkeys. But her stomach remained tight and her head felt a little dizzy as she started down the long walk to the school door.

Adalyn was keeping her head down as she always did, when suddenly she heard a friendly voice.

"Good morning, Adalyn," said Mrs. Kelly. "Welcome back."

Adalyn's heart felt warm and grateful as she raised her head to see her teacher … and sitting right next to Mrs. Kelly, Clare. Clare's tail was wagging so hard it seemed to shake her whole body. Clare instantly came over and nuzzled Adalyn's leg and licked her hand. Gradually, Adalyn felt her stomach relax.

Chapter Thirteen: Henry

Adalyn started her day in Mrs. Kelly's room. This was called her "processing" time. This was private time with Mrs. Kelly to talk about what had happened, how to do a better job of keeping those angry words inside her head, and how to use her relaxation tools before her worries get too wild and unruly.

Clare watched and listened carefully. She knew about fear in the wild, and instinctively knew that when facing a fearful animal, it was best to get very small and make herself feel relaxed. She knew she needed to learn everything she could about human worries so she could help Adalyn.

One thing Clare was really good at was what the dogs back home called "super sense." She could almost always tell if humans were having fearful thoughts, even if their faces didn't look that way. They smelled different.

"I think you should start with Mr. Spencer's room," Mrs. Kelly suggested to Adalyn. "You can go over the work you did on your report and say hello to the animals before going to Miss Thomas' room."

Adalyn was still feeling nervous as she and Clare started out for Mr. Spencer's room. "I'm capable!" she said in a whisper.

This was called an affirmation, and Mrs. Kelly wanted her to practice saying it to herself over and over. It meant that she was strong and capable of controlling her worries. When she said it, she was supposed to think about her calmest thoughts. She looked down at Clare.

"Will you be my affirmation, Clare?" she asked quietly. "Thinking about you is one of the very calmest thoughts I have."

Clare thought that if she could do the Weasel War Dance, she would be doing it right now. She wagged her tail, and looked right up at Adalyn's face to send a strong, friendly message.

When they got to Mr. Spencer's room, the first person Clare saw was Henry. Clare could hardly believe her luck – here was one of the humans she had picked for Adalyn's pack.

She ran up to Henry and licked his hand. She then looked back at Adalyn with excitement, only to see her walk right past Henry without even noticing him! Adalyn was headed straight toward Mr. Spencer and had already started telling him about the changes she had made on her paper.

"I clarified the Kiwi mother's role prior to the laying of the egg as well as the father's role during incubation," Adalyn reported with enthusiasm.

"Excellent," said Mr. Spencer. "And may I say, I am so happy to see you back at school. I missed you."

Adalyn was speechless. She had been hoping that Mr. Spencer didn't think she was a criminal, but she never expected this!

Meanwhile, Clare continued to stand next to Henry, who scratched her ears and watched as Adalyn told Mr. Spencer about her report. He too had a report that won an award and was going to the state fair. His report was about the ten most extraordinary lakes in the world.

Suddenly, Adalyn turned and looked at Clare and Henry.

"Do you know Clare?" she asked Henry.

"Do you know which is the highest fresh water lake in the world?" Henry replied, immediately realizing it was the lamest thing he had ever said in his whole entire life.

But Adalyn didn't seem to mind, and went straight on to say, "That would be Lake Titicaca, located in South America, on the border between Bolivia and Peru."

There was a brief moment of silence as Henry and Adalyn both realized they had almost had a conversation. Then there was another moment, when they both realized that Adalyn had just said the word "Titicaca" out loud.

Henry started to giggle, and then Adalyn giggled, too. Finally, Mr. Spencer could not help himself and started to laugh. Soon all three were laughing. They laughed, and laughed, and laughed.

Chapter Fourteen: Taking Perspective

"That was a bit of brilliant work on your part," Orin said to Clare. "Henry is a perfect choice for Adalyn's pack.

"Thank you," replied Clare proudly.

"I heard Henry invite Adalyn to eat lunch with him," added Alejandro. "Unfortunately, that's not a good idea."

"But that's what we do with our packs," explained Clare. "Eating is just about the happiest thing one can do with pack mates."

"You think like that because you are a dog who loves food as much as life itself," snapped Alejandro. "But think for a minute about Adalyn's perspective!"

"What is a perspective?" asked Clare.

"Putting yourself in another person's shoes," offered Pixie.

"Being sensitive to another person's experience," added Julia.

"Last year, Adalyn had problems with the smells in the cafeteria," said Nancy, "so Mrs.

Kelly suggested that she only eat in the cafeteria on Bag Lunch Fridays."

"That is why she usually eats lunch in the library office," explained Orin.

"The smell of cooking food was making Adalyn nervous," elaborated Pixie; "it made it hard for her to handle even little problems."

"What?" burst out Clare, totally amazed at the thought that the smell of food could be anything but utterly sublime.

"I could snap a lunch lady's ear off in one second!" yelled Carter.

"The smell of cooked meat makes me go crazy, too," said Alejandro. "It wouldn't matter if I had a whole herd of other guinea pigs backing me up!"

"Please help me understand," pleaded Clare, and that is how she came to hear Alejandro's story.

Alejandro was originally from Peru, South America. Here he lived with a herd of other guinea pigs, at the base of the Andes Mountains.

One day, they were surprised by a group of humans, who captured Alejandro and his friends. The humans put them in cages and brought them to town to be a part of the world-famous Guinea Pig Festival.

At first, Alejandro explained, it seemed like fun. They were the guests of honor at a huge party. Alejandro was dressed up in a fedora and pants, and he was given all the corn he could eat. But gradually his herd started to mysteriously disappear, one at a time, which made him nervous and very uncomfortable. Soon he started to smell the putrid scent of meat cooking. Alejandro could hardly believe what was happening: Not only were he and his herd the guests of honor, they were also **the meal!**

Alejandro was in the arms of a little girl when he realized what was going on. Hearing him shriek out in horror, the girl got scared and threw him into the air. Luckily, he landed right on top of a pile of burlap sacks filled with coffee beans. The sacks were on a vendor's cart bound for Lima, on the coast of the Pacific Ocean.

Soon he was on his way! During the trip to Lima, Alejandro burrowed his way into one of the burlap sacks for safety. When the cart arrived at the docks, Alejandro's sack was thrown aboard a ship bound for Los Angeles, California.

The first night aboard the ship, Alejandro cautiously crept out of his burlap sack to try to figure out where he was. Almost immediately, he was greeted by some of the resident rats. They were very kind to him, and showed him how to creep into the galley where the sailors ate their meals, to find good things to eat.

Alejandro and the rats talked into the wee hours of the night, comparing life stories and sharing interesting bits about the differences between living on land and living on the sea. Among many new things, he learned that a bunch of rats were called a "mischief." In exchange, he told the rats that a bunch of guinea pigs were called a "herd."

The days aboard the ship were long and bumpy. Alejandro spent most of his time scavenging about, always looking for something to chew on. On the third day, the ship ran into a terrible storm, and Alejandro found himself being thrown from one end of the ship to the other.

Terrified of what might happen, he decided to return to the safety of his burlap sack. But on the way back, some of the cargo boxes got loose and began to slide across the hold of the ship. Alejandro scrambled harder, but he was not strong enough to get out of the way, so one of the heavy boxes smashed right into him, severing his right front leg.

"Help," he cried, as he winced with unbearable pain.

Within seconds of hearing his call, six of his new rat friends came to his rescue. The strong ship rats pulled Alejandro back to his burlap sack, and then they gnawed off some pieces of the burlap material and stuffed them into Alejandro's bloody stump to stop the bleeding.

For eight days, Alejandro rested in his sack of coffee beans. In the meantime, his new seafaring rat friends never let him down, but brought him food to eat and interesting things to chew on.

Finally, after eleven days at sea, the ship docked in Los Angeles, USA. By this time, Alejandro felt well enough to venture out onto to the gangplank, where he found a place to rest in the sunshine. After being cooped up in the dark of the burlap sack, he took some time to enjoy the warm sun and the smells of this new world before he began to look for lunch.

As he looked around at all the boats and activities in the harbor, he noticed a patch of green grass just under the end of the gangplank, and carefully began making his way to the land below.

After a satisfying lunch of fresh green grass, Alejandro looked around at all the sailboats in the harbor. Soon he noticed a 38-footer named Andy's Appetite. He wondered to himself if this was a boat from his beloved Andes mountain range.

Alejandro was terribly homesick, so he decided to take a chance and made his way over to the boat. He boldly boarded by making a somewhat awkward three-legged leap from the dock to the bow of the boat. But as soon as his three legs hit the deck, he was covered by a wooden crate!

"Oh no," he thought. "Will my bad luck ever end?"

"What did you catch, Andy?" asked Joyce McGrade.

"Not sure," answered her husband, Andy. "It's too fat to be a rat and too small to be a cat."

"Let me take a look," said Joyce, as she peered through the slates of the crate. "Oh my, I think it's a guinea pig, but I believe he's hurt."

Listening to the conversation around him, Alejandro slowly began to put the pieces together. He figured out that the boat was named after Andy McGrade, who was a retired custodian from Minnesota traveling around the world with his wife, Joyce. Joyce was a retired elementary school teacher, so she knew a lot about guinea pigs, and she turned out to be a great nurse for Alejandro.

When Joyce realized that poor Alejandro only had three legs and that he might not be able to survive on his own, she decided to take him back home on their next road trip to Minnesota. Joyce had a friend named Thomas Spencer, who was a science teacher and who she was certain would love to care for a three-legged guinea pig.

"Wow," said Clare, riveted by the account of Alejandro's terrifying experience. "I think I'm beginning to understand."

"Perspective is the big enchilada," continued Alejandro. "If Adalyn can't handle the smells, the cafeteria might be a hard place to be, even with a pack, a herd, or a mischief."

Chapter Fifteen: The Bail-out

Ever since they had met that day in Mr. Spencer's room, Henry and Adalyn had talked almost every single day. They talked about the interesting animals native to China and about the surface area of the Caspian Sea. They talked about their favorite elements on the periodic table and Henry's collection of rhinoceros beetles. After four years, seven months, and twenty days, Adalyn had finally found a friend!

Aside from talking about favorite things, friends usually like to eat lunch together, so when Henry asked Adalyn if she wanted to eat lunch at his table, it felt like panic.

"I hate the cafeteria!" Adalyn declared in a strong voice. "It's loud, it stinks, and everyone moves too fast!"

"But ...," started Henry, "I was just suggesting ..."

"OK, OK. I will try," Adalyn softened.

"Cool. I sit at the table near the stage," said Henry.

It was two days later, and Adalyn was meeting Henry for lunch. On one hand, she was pretty nervous about the sounds and smells of the cafeteria; on the other hand, it would give her a chance to tell Henry all about the article she had just read concerning the endangered red colobus monkeys of Ghana, Africa.

Before heading to lunch, Adalyn walked Clare to the science room. There were certain places in the school building where Clare was not allowed to go, and the cafeteria was one of those places.

"Wait here and take a nap or something," Adalyn said to her. "I'll be back after lunch, and we'll play some ball." Then she walked out of the science room, closing the door behind her.

The minute she heard the door shut, Clare freaked out.

"Oh no!" she shrieked. "Adalyn is on her way to the cafeteria. I'm not allowed, and now the door is closed!!"

"Calm down, child," said Julia in her Trinidadian rhythm.

"How can I calm down when I'm flunking my next big test?" cried Clare. "I'm dropping the ball! I'm hopeless!!"

"That door never closes all the way," said Julia. "You just need to push it."

Clare looked hopefully at Julia, took a deep breath, and pushed the door with her nose. Sure enough, it was open, and soon Clare was in the hallway, on her way to the cafeteria.

In the meantime, Adalyn was walking down the hall toward the cafeteria, repeating, "I am capable" to herself under her breath. She knew she would need to be prepared, using all the calming tools she had.

Despite everything, the moment Adalyn walked into the cafeteria, she felt her stomach tighten. She closed her eyes, and took a slow, deep breath, only to breathe in the smell of a whole bunch of macaroni pie, canned peas, and Chef's Surprise!

Adalyn immediately started to feel sick to her stomach, and noticed the tension rising in her body. She knew this feeling well; her worries were getting too big! It was time for what Mrs. Kelly called "a bail-out plan." Having tried everything else, Adalyn turned around and quickly walked out of the cafeteria.

🐾

Adalyn moved into the hallway and put her back against the wall, easing herself to the floor. Soon Clare snuggled in close to Adalyn, licked her hand, and smelled her breath. Clare had been waiting at the doorway, making herself small and calm. She had been watching closely, and could smell the fear as it began to take hold of Adalyn.

"Snagly," said Adalyn with a smile. "Being near you really is my calmest thing."

"Oh. There you are."

She suddenly heard Henry's voice, as he was also coming out into the hallway. "One minute

I saw you in the cafeteria, and the next minute you were gone."

"Oh, hi, Henry," answered Adalyn. "I was feeling sorry for poor Clare. She isn't allowed in the cafeteria."

"Poor pup. Maybe we could eat somewhere else?" suggested Henry.

"How about the library office," Adalyn quickly responded. "Miss Dudley loves dogs."

"Cool," Henry said. "I'll grab my lunch."

A minute later, they were all three on their way to the library.

"So, have you heard about the discovery of new planets outside of our solar system?" Henry asked. "The scientists are calling them Super-Earths!"

Chapter Sixteen: A Science Club

The following week, Adalyn and Henry were meeting with Mr. Spencer in the science room, when Mr. Peterson walked in with Mr. Hirtle.

Clare, who had been sleeping by the window in a warm sunbeam, immediately woke up and looked at Adalyn. She smelled fear.

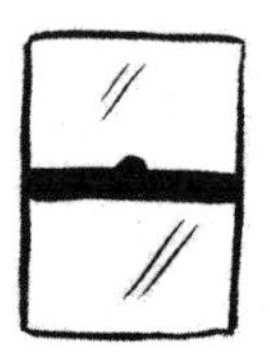

Mr. Peterson motioned to Mr. Spencer, silently indicating that he would like to speak with him in private. After excusing himself from Adalyn and Henry, Mr. Spencer walked over to greet his guests.

"Have you met Randy Hirtle?" asked Mr. Peterson. "He is our student teacher this semester; he has been working in Miss Thomas' room."

Mr. Spencer nodded and reached out his hand to Mr. Hirtle. "Nice to meet you," he said.

"Thanks," said Mr. Hirtle. "I've been hoping to get a chance to work with science. It was my specialty at the university."

"That's great," said Mr. Spencer with a smile. "We can always use more science teachers."

"I was thinking," continued Mr. Peterson, "that Randy could finish off the year under your supervision, maybe coordinating the science fair winners and helping with the trip to the state fair."

Meanwhile, Clare had slowly begun to inch her way over to Adalyn, who was sitting with her mouth hanging open.

"This can't be happening," thought Adalyn. "The science room is my refuge, my safe zone, my passion. Mr. Hirtle is an imposter! He's not a scientist! He's not even a real teacher, and he swallows children whole!"

As Adalyn felt her worries rising, Clare was instantly at her side, nose on her hand. Adalyn began to relax.

"Wow," thought Clare, "that worked really well."

"Wow," thought Adalyn, "that worked really well."

When Adalyn finally looked up, Mr. Spencer was walking with Mr. Hirtle across the room toward Henry and Adalyn.

"Henry," Mr. Spencer started. "This is Mr. Hirtle; he will be working with us on the science projects." He then turned to Adalyn and added, "Adalyn, you must know Mr. Hirtle from your classroom."

There was an awkward moment between Adalyn and Mr. Hirtle. It felt like tension in the air, or some kind of bad energy. Clare felt it immediately, and remained alert and on duty.

"Hello, Adalyn," said Mr. Hirtle, "I didn't realize you liked science."

"Oh yes," interrupted Mr. Spencer. "Adalyn is one of our school winners for the science fair. She is on her way to becoming a brilliant scientist."

Still unable to think of anything to say, Adalyn remained silent.

Finally, Mr. Spencer and Mr. Hirtle walked across the room to discuss their plans.

Adalyn looked at Henry, "Can you believe it?"

"Believe what?" asked Henry.

"That wicked Mr. Hirtle is pretending to be a scientist," Adalyn sneered.

"Maybe he is a scientist," suggested Henry.

"He is not!" said Adalyn, feeling her tension rise again.

Just then, Mr. Spencer hurried back to their worktable. "Mr. Hirtle just had a great idea!" he announced. "He suggested we form an after-school science club. What do you think?"

"That is an amazing idea," said Henry with excitement.

"Are you sure Mr. Hirtle thought of it?" asked Adalyn.

"Absolutely," said Mr. Spencer. "He told me that when he was a kid, he always wished someone would start a science club in his school."

Hearing their conversation, Mr. Hirtle walked toward the group. "Yes," he continued, "I was thinking that a science club would be a great place to meet other kids who like science."

Every single animal ear in the science room heard that one, and Clare looked at Mr. Hirtle with new admiration.

Henry immediately announced, "I know that my friend Vicente would like to be in a science club."

"Great," said Mr. Hirtle." Henry and Adalyn, why don't you both think about other students who might like to come, and I will do the paperwork necessary to officially start a club."

Adalyn wasn't sure about this. On one hand, having a science club at school was the best thing to ever happen in her whole school life. On the other hand, it was Mr. Hirtle, and he was mean and wicked, Adalyn was absolutely sure of that.

Chapter Seventeen: Kirsten

Adalyn thought about the science club while she was putting books back on the library shelves. She could hardly believe there was going to be a special club devoted to simply talking about science. There was nothing she loved more than to talk and think about science, especially animals.

Adalyn closed her eyes and thought about Costa Rica, and then whispered, "the howler monkey, the spider monkey, and the squirrel monkey."

Meanwhile, Clare watched the activities in the library from Miss Dudley's check-out desk. She watched the children come and go, and after a short while, she noticed the "star girl" walk in. The girl came in alone and sat down by herself in the far corner of the room.

"This is my moment," thought Clare. "It is now or never!"

Then she walked over to the star girl's table, wagging her tail to show her most friendly enthusiasm.

The girl saw Clare approaching and smiled.

"Hi, Clare!" she said.

Even though she was close by, Adalyn didn't notice; she was way too busy thinking of more mammals found in Central America.

🐾

When it was time for Adalyn to go back to Miss Thomas' room, she looked around for Clare. She finally caught sight of her lying under the back table, next to a strange girl. Adalyn walked toward Clare and noticed that the girl at the table was studying a chart in a star atlas.

"Do you know Clare?" Adalyn asked.

"Yes," answered the girl, looking up.

Adalyn continued, "Do you like astronomy?"

"Yes," said the girl shyly.

After a moment of silence, the girl added, "I love astronomy and constellations, and basically all celestial objects."

Adalyn was silent for another prolonged moment, and then she asked, "Would you like to be in a science club?"

"Yes," answered the girl promptly.

Adalyn looked away, unsure of what to do next. Clare wagged her tail and licked the girl's hand. Then she ran to Adalyn, wagged her tail again and also licked her hand.

Adalyn laughed and said, "I think Clare is introducing us. My name is Adalyn."

"My name is Kirsten."

"Hello, Kirsten," said Adalyn.

"Hello, Adalyn," said Kirsten.

🐾

The next week, Mr. Hirtle welcomed five students to his newly formed science club. There were Adalyn, Henry, Kirsten, and Vicente, and a sixth grader named Miles.

"Well," started Mr. Hirtle. "I know that all of you have your own favorite science topics and that we all love to talk about what interests us. So, I have created a schedule of topics for the final five weeks of school.

Adalyn listened as he told the group that the first topic would be endangered animals, then geographic anomalies, followed by meteorology, then parallel universes, and ending the year by giving the science fair winners an opportunity to practice defending their papers.

Despite her feelings about Mr. Hirtle and the science club, Adalyn eagerly started off the discussion by talking about snow leopards and mountain gorillas. Henry jumped in to talk about leatherback sea turtles and giant pandas.

Mr. Hirtle added a discussion about the northern white rhinoceros, and Vicente mentioned the plight of the red wolf. Miles, who was a birder, reminded everyone of the dangers of losing the henslow sparrow, the burrowing owl, and the piping plover, right there in Minnesota.

After the meeting, Mr. Hirtle asked Adalyn to wait in the room because he wanted to talk to her.

Still glowing from the great factual discussion they had just had, Adalyn stopped and waited patiently as the others left the room.

"Adalyn," started Mr. Hirtle. "I believe I owe you an apology."

"What?" Adalyn blurted out.

"I judged you, and that was wrong. Teachers shouldn't judge their students."

Adalyn was speechless!

"We all face things in life that are difficult, and you deserve all the support you can get," he continued. "It wasn't right for me to question your plan the way I did that day in class when you had to leave the room."

Adalyn started to feel dizzy. Could this be true? Was this what an apology felt like? Was Mr. Hirtle actually nice, or was this a trick? Her head started to hurt as she found herself questioning the few things she thought she knew about people.

Because she could think of nothing else to say, she turned and quietly started to walk out of the room. But when she reached the door, she remembered one of her reminder signs. She turned back around and said, "Thank you, Mr. Hirtle."

Chapter Eighteen: Mr. Hirtle

"Hooray!"
"Way to go!"
"You rock!"

Clare was in the science room, and all of the animals were celebrating her huge success.

"We are so proud of you, Clare," started Nancy.

"We most certainly are," added Orin.

Clare was overwhelmed with pride and happiness. She had done a good job. She knew it, and her friends knew it, too.

"Thank you," she said. "Success feels so much better than failure."

"You must be very proud of Adalyn, too," added Alejandro.

"Oh yes," replied Clare. "She is working so hard to learn about being social; she practices her relaxation every morning, and she has smiled almost every day."

"Child, I almost choked when I heard Mr. Hirtle suggest the science club!" remarked Julia.

"Great minds think alike," said Orin. "I am liking Mr. Hirtle more and more every day."

"Me too," said Pixie. "I love how he walks past our cages every morning and says hello to each of us."

"I love that he knows how important it is to have two or more guinea pigs," Alejandro went on. "He told Mr. Spencer that guinea pigs need other guinea pigs to cuddle with, and he's bringing in a partner for me!"

"He also knew that rats need time alone, away from the excitement of a school classroom," Nancy interjected, "so he's building a hideout for our cage."

"I think he's a lot like Adalyn," said Carter.

The room suddenly went quiet. All of the animals looked at Carter, shocked that he had just said something kind of smart. Given his belligerent disposition, he was rarely included in the animal discussions.

Clare was the first to speak up, "I was thinking the same thing. He doesn't like to eat with the other teachers."

"That's true; he prefers to eat in the science room and talk to us," added Pixie.

"He talks to himself when the other humans aren't around," said Nancy. "Adalyn does that, too."

"Carter," said Orin, "congratulations on your brilliant observation."

Carter blushed and quickly pulled his head into his shell. Nobody had ever called him brilliant before.

Clare was thinking about what Carter had said. Maybe Mr. Hirtle had said mean things to Adalyn because he wasn't very good with people either. Maybe Mr. Hirtle wanted a science club because he liked to talk about science more than anything else. Maybe the science club would become Mr. Hirtle's pack, too.

Chapter Nineteen: A Natural Disaster

The following week at the science club, the discussion was about "geographic anomalies," which refers to surprising facts about land, positions of land, or shapes of land.

Henry did most of the talking, because geographic anomalies were one of his favorite things. He spent a good part of the hour talking about how the top part of Minnesota and the town of Point Roberts, Washington, are both in the United States, but are only accessible by land if you go through Canada.

It was a fun topic for everyone, and Mr. Hirtle pulled down the world map to show different locations as people mentioned them. At one point, everyone was yelling out geographic anomalies, one after another.

"The Atlantic end of the Panama Canal is west of the Pacific end," claimed Vicente.

"There is an 800-mile wide mass of hot rock under the water near Hawaii," said Miles.

"Calais, Maine, is closer to Dublin, Ireland, than it is to San Diego, California," added Adalyn.

"The Olympus Mons on Mars is the largest known mountain in the solar system," shouted Kirsten.

By the end of the discussion, everyone was interrupting each other with bigger and better facts, and everyone was laughing and having a great time.

Before they left for the day, Mr. Hirtle announced that the following week, in honor of the meteorology topic, they would all be going to the Science Museum of Minnesota to see an exhibit called Nature Unleashed: Inside Natural Disasters. Adalyn could hardly wait a whole week. This was the best thing to happen to her in her whole school life!

On the day of the field trip, Adalyn arrived at school early, her backpack filled with special things that she and her father had selected. There was a pen and pad to write down fun facts; two granola bars for a snack; and the *Rough Guide to Weather* that Adalyn and her father had read together, with dog-eared pages where they had questions. Adalyn's father had also given her a cell phone to use for the day, telling her to call him immediately if she saw something awesome.

Mrs. Kelly and Clare weren't at school yet, so Adalyn went down to the science room to talk with Mr. Hirtle about the trip. When Adalyn arrived at the room, she saw a note on the door. She looked closely and read aloud, "Science Club, please go to Mr. Peterson's office as soon as you get to school." This was not good, thought Adalyn, and she could feel her worries starting to grow.

As she walked down the hallway toward Mr. Peterson's office, she found herself listing the whale species found in the Bay of Fundy, Canada. When she stopped at the office door, she whispered "piping plover," a term she had been saying on and off since she had heard Miles say it at the first science club meeting.

Inside the office, Adalyn saw that Henry, Vicente, and Miles were already there. She took a seat next to Miles and tried not to think about what was happening. When Kirsten arrived, Mr. Peterson joined them at the table and delivered the disappointing news.

"Mr. Hirtle has been called out of town for a family emergency," Mr. Peterson said in a calm, steady voice. "The trip to the science museum has been postponed."

"Dang," said Henry.

"Oh, drat," said Kirsten

"Nooooo!!!!" screamed Adalyn, "This can't be happening! This is a disaster! I can't stand it!"

Mr. Peterson was taken aback, as were Adalyn's friends. Nobody in the room had ever witnessed Adalyn lose control, and everyone thought it was a little scary.

"Now, Adalyn," started Mr. Peterson.

"Don't say another word!" screamed Adalyn. "Don't say one more thing, or you will live to regret it!"

Chapter Twenty: Good Ideas

Mr. Peterson asked Henry, Miles, Kirsten, and Vicente to leave the room. He then paged Mrs. Kelly, and tried to remain calm while he waited for her guidance in dealing with Adalyn.

When Mrs. Kelly and Clare arrived outside the office, they could hear Adalyn inside. She was yelling out the names of marine animals found in Antarctica. And as they opened the door, they could see her pacing back and forth, pounding her fists against the air, as if boxing some invisible opponent.

Clare quickly made herself very small, and crept closer to Adalyn. Mrs. Kelly began to take very slow, deep breaths, and handed Mr. Peterson a note that said, "Don't look directly at Adalyn."

As Mr. Peterson watched the scene unfold, he was fascinated by what was happening. Mrs. Kelly and Clare were so calm; he could actually feel the tension in the room diffusing. At the same time, both Mrs. Kelly and Clare were very slowly moving closer to Adalyn, and they kept breathing very slowly.

When Mrs. Kelly finally spoke, he noticed that it was in a very low and very calm voice. She simply said, "I know."

The next time she spoke, she said, "You can do it," followed shortly thereafter by, "I will support you."

Finally, Adalyn stopped pacing and collapsed to the floor. Clare went up to her and nuzzled her hair. Mrs. Kelly sat down a few inches from Adalyn, continuing her silent, slow breathing.

Soon Adalyn started to cry, and Mrs. Kelly now moved in to offer her a hug. Clare held her position so that her body was touching Adalyn's. Witnessing all this, Mr. Peterson seemed overcome with emotion.

Suddenly, the disaster was over. Adalyn had calmed down, Clare was holding her ground at Adalyn's side, and Mrs. Kelly was ready to talk with Mr. Peterson.

A little while later, when Adalyn was calm enough to do some silent reading on her own, Mr. Peterson and Mrs. Kelly moved to a private office. Mr. Peterson wanted Mrs. Kelly to help him understand what he had just seen.

"I think that Adalyn's loss of control comes from her frustration with people," explained Mrs. Kelly. "People make her nervous, and when something goes wrong, her anxiety gets bigger than she can handle."

"We have been practicing relaxation so that Adalyn can learn to handle life's disappointments without losing control of her emotions," she added.

"Why didn't you want me to look at her?" asked Mr. Peterson curiously.

"Because looking at someone in the eyes can feel very threatening," said Mrs. Kelly. "Looking at someone when they are really upset can make their anxiety even worse."

"As you might have noticed, I was trying to help Adalyn calm down by remaining very calm myself," continued Mrs. Kelly. "Clare seems to do this naturally, which is why she is so helpful to Adalyn."

Mr. Peterson asked, "Would you be willing to teach the other teachers how to do what you just did with Adalyn?"

"I would be happy to," said Mrs. Kelly.

Mrs. Kelly walked Adalyn and Clare back to her room, so that Adalyn could spend some time with Clare in the pop-up tent.

Once inside the tent, Clare looked out the specially designed peek hole, and there was Mrs. Kelly, doing what looked like the Weasel War Dance.

Chapter Twenty-One: Friendship

A few days after Adalyn's difficult moment, Mrs. Kelly suggested that they have a special meeting with her science club. She could help Adalyn explain what had happened in the office, and Adalyn could share how she was learning to relax.

After giving this idea some thought, Adalyn asked, "Will it help them not be afraid of me?"

"I think so," answered Mrs. Kelly.

They had the meeting the next day. Mrs. Kelly decided to start by asking the kids if they had any questions or comments about what they experienced when Adalyn had lost control.

"I was thinking," started Miles, "that Adalyn was probably feeling what I was feeling, only about ten times more."

"That is 100% brilliant," replied Mrs. Kelly.

"My little brother has problems with anxieties too," said Kirsten. "Sometimes he screams when my mom changes her mind about something we had planned to do."

"Then you must know a lot about anxiety," said Mrs. Kelly.

"I don't think I have big emotions, said Henry, "but sometimes world events, like war, give me a stomachache."

"That might be a message from your emotions telling your brain that war makes you upset," suggested Mrs. Kelly.

"I almost punched someone," said Vicente, "who teased us about having a science club."

"How did you stop yourself?" asked Mrs. Kelly.

"I walked away really fast before my fist took control," Vicente answered.

"What an excellent thing to do. Like Miles said, Adalyn's emotions are about ten times bigger than most kids', so walking away isn't an easy thing for her to do," Mrs. Kelly commented.

"I'm learning how to relax my body," explained Adalyn, "and walking away quickly is one of the strategies I use before my emotions get too big."

"Also, Clare helps Adalyn to stay in control of her emotions," added Mrs. Kelly.

"I know about that," said Kirsten. "Dogs have good social instincts, and if a person pets a dog, it can make the person calm."

"Cool," added Henry. "I saw a science special about that on TV one time, but I never connected it to Clare and Adalyn."

Mrs. Kelly was feeling so proud and grateful to these students. Not only did they appreciate Adalyn's love of science, they also understood her emotional challenge, actually better than some of the teachers.

"Thank you," she finally said to the group. "Thank you for being such caring friends."

The school year was almost over. This made all the students happy, but summer vacation was the hardest time for the science room animals. Mr. Spencer couldn't take everyone home with him, so he had to find other teachers to be summertime foster parents.

Clare was terribly upset. She wouldn't see her friends for three whole months. Besides, she had overheard Adalyn telling Kirsten that she would be going to Nova Scotia for an entire month with her family.

"Nova Scotia!" Clare complained. "That's like three days riding in a car or three months of walking, just to get there!"

"It will be okay," Nancy reassured her. "Summer vacation is just a part of life here at school. Besides, you will see Adalyn at the state fair in August."

"Tell her the surprise," prompted Orin.

"OK," said Nancy. "Mrs. Kelly has agreed to take Orin and me for the summer. We're going to your house!"

Clare was so happy she could hardly believe it. It felt like chasing squirrels or finding a piece of cheddar cheese on the kitchen floor.

"Walter and I are going with Mr. Hirtle," said Alejandro. Walter was Mr. Hirtle's guinea pig, and the newest addition to the science room.

"I'll be going with Mr. Peterson," said Pixie." His children ask for me every summer."

"What about Julia and Carter?" Clare asked.

"Well, now that is the best story of all," said Orin. "They are both going home."

"Mr. Spencer is taking me back to my beloved Trinidad," said Julia, too choked up with happiness to say more.

"It is a great story!" said Pixie. "When Mr. Spencer heard Miles' science fair report about the twenty-one species of hummingbirds found in Trinidad, he decided to go there. He found out that the best place to see hummingbirds was in the Trinidadian rainforest at a sanctuary called Asa Wright. When he contacted the sanctuary office, he found out that there were motmot birds living there as well. He decided to take Julia with him and release her to live in the rainforest!"

"Oh, Julia," said Clare. "I am so happy for you."

"And Carter is going home to the Boundary Waters," said Alejandro, "The math teacher is going up there on a canoe trip, and has agreed to take Carter with him."

Clare was feeling happy and sad, and nervous and excited all at once. On one hand, she would miss Julia very much; on the other hand, she knew how much Julia wanted to go home. On one hand, she would miss seeing everyone every day; on the other hand, Nancy and Orin were coming to her house. On one hand, she would miss Adalyn; on the other hand, it was only three months until the Minnesota State Fair.

Chapter Twenty-Two: The Fair

"I will hate the smells, and the heat, and the crowds, and the food, and the noise," announced Adalyn to her mom and dad.

"You're right. It's going to be a challenge for sure," agreed her mother.

"But it'll be an interesting adventure," added her father.

All three were getting ready for their first-ever full day at the state fair. Mrs. Kelly had called the night before and arranged to meet them at the main entrance to the fair. She had even obtained special permission to bring Clare.

"Henry and Miles will be there to defend their papers," announced Adalyn, "and Kirsten and Vicente are coming to support us!"

Adalyn's parents silently swelled with pride and happiness at hearing their beautiful, smart, and precious daughter talk about her friends.

It was just after 10:00 a.m. when Adalyn, her parents, Mrs. Kelly, and Clare walked into the education building at the fair. Miles and Vicente were already there, and were the first to notice Clare walking towards them.

"Hey, Clare," they yelled out in unison.

Clare was so happy to see everyone that she almost missed the lump of macaroni and cheese lying under the poetry exhibit.

"Hello, Vicente; hi, Miles," said Adalyn. "Have you seen Henry and Kirsten?"

"Haven't looked," said Vicente.

"They were here," said Miles. "I'm sure they'll show up soon; the awards will be posted before noon."

Just then, Henry and Kirsten entered the building. As they approached Adalyn, she noticed that they each had what looked like big tattoos on their faces.

"What happened to your faces?"

"We found a face painter, and I decided on Einstein's famous formula $E = mc^2$," said Henry laughing.

Kirsten, who had a big capital H on her cheek, said, "And I decided on the symbol for hydrogen, since it makes up much of Jupiter, which is my favorite planet."

Adalyn smiled; she really liked her friends.

Just then, Mr. Spencer joined the group.

"I am so proud to have three students represented in the state fair this year. Regardless of what happens, I want you all to know, I am bursting with pride."

"I'm sure I'll win the grand prize," announced Adalyn. "My report is excellent, and you said yourself that it is certainly worthy."

Mr. Spencer sent a quick message to Mrs. Kelly with his eyes. He was a little worried about how Adalyn might react if things didn't work out as she expected.

Picking up on Mr. Spencer's look, Mrs. Kelly asked Adalyn if she would help her take Clare for a walk.

"Sure," said Adalyn, and off they went, away from the crowd.

On the way to the grassy area where Clare could play, they passed a big white tent with a sign that said "Meditation Tent."

"Wow," said Adalyn. "What's that?"

"Looks like a public pop-up tent!" said Mrs. Kelly. "There are obviously a lot of people who need to take breaks from the noise and smells and excitement of the fair."

"I never thought about other people having worries. I thought I was the only one," said Adalyn.

"Oh my," replied Mrs. Kelly. "There are thousands of other people who need help with their worries."

"Snagly," whispered Adalyn.

"By the way, I think we should work on your relaxation before we go back to the education building," said Mrs. Kelly.

"Because I'm so excited?" asked Adalyn.

"Well," said Mrs. Kelly, "because you are excited and because you are anticipating."

"What do you mean 'anticipating'?" asked Adalyn.

"In your mind, you are telling yourself that you are going to get the grand prize," said Mrs. Kelly.

"Yes! I can hardly wait!"

"But what if you get second place, or honorable mention?"

"But I won't. I will most likely be getting the grand prize," replied Adalyn.

"Let's take a deep breath together," suggested Mrs. Kelly. "Then, let's close our eyes and think about your affirmation thoughts."

Adalyn followed Mrs. Kelly through the familiar routine as Clare got close … and very small.

Then, in a soft and gentle voice, Mrs. Kelly explained that Adalyn might get honorable mention. She added that having a paper at the state fair was already like winning.

"I imagine the results are being announced right about now," said Mrs. Kelly. "Do you think you should go back to the education building to find out, or would you rather wait here with Clare while I go and find out?"

Adalyn gave this question some serious thought, and then said, "I think I would like to go with you. I think I am capable."

"What are you going to do if you don't win?" asked Mrs. Kelly.

"Close my eyes, take a deep breath, use my affirmations, recite my lists, and look for Clare."

"Good plan," said Mrs. Kelly as they walked back in to join the others.

"There you are," called out Mr. Hirtle. "I was just about to have a short meeting with my science club."

"When I was your age," he started, "I wrote a science paper that was judged worthy of the state fair."

"Did you win the grand prize? I bet you won the grand prize," blurted Adalyn.

"I thought I was going to win the grand prize," answered Mr. Hirtle. "Actually I was sure of it, but I didn't win."

"Were you very sad?" asked Kirsten.

"At first, I had too many emotions to decide how I felt," admitted Mr. Hirtle, "so I went into the bathroom and had a little cry."

"Get out!" yelled Vicente. "You didn't cry, did you?"

"As a matter of fact, I did," said Mr. Hirtle. Then he went on to explain that sometimes strong emotions come out of nowhere and that almost anybody might cry if they are taken by surprise, or if they are terribly disappointed.

"You know what I wish had happened that day?" he asked.

"That you got the grand prize," Adalyn guessed.

"No. Actually I won other prizes," said Mr. Hirtle. "On that day, I wish someone had been with me. You guys are like the biggest grand-prize winners of all. You have two friends, four moms, four dads, three teachers, and a dog here to give you hugs, kisses, and high fives, no matter what happens."

Mr. Hirtle was suddenly interrupted by commotion in the back of the building. The list of award winners was being posted!

With almost lightening speed, Adalyn ran over to the announcement board, standing with her arms outstretched and her nose less than six inches from the posted list. She was just staring.

Suddenly, she was surrounded by all of the other participants, everyone looking for their name, their child's name, or their student's name. Some people squealed with delight, others walked away slowly, their heads down.

Soon Adalyn was the only person left. She had not moved an inch. Her arms were still outstretched, and she was still staring at the list of names. But inside her head, almost on automatic pilot, she had begun listing the large mammals of Botswana.

Clare could sense the worry in the room, so she slowly approached Adalyn, trying to smell the fear that usually accompanied Adalyn's big emotions. Adalyn was taking slow, deep breaths and mumbling quietly, but Clare did not smell fear. She calmly nuzzled Adalyn's leg.

Sensing Clare by her side, Adalyn looked down. Then she brought one hand down and began to scratch behind Clare's ear. She could feel her worries were easing, and she thought to herself, "I ***am*** capable."

Then Adalyn turned to face Miles. "You won the grand prize."

"Yes, I did," he said.

"Congratulations," Adalyn said as she reached out her hand.

Then she turned to Mrs. Kelly and said, "I got an honorable mention."

"I know," said Mrs. Kelly.

"I was practically 100% certain that I would win the grand prize," continued Adalyn.

"I know," replied Mrs. Kelly.

At this point, Kirsten, Henry, and Vicente slowly eased in for what could be considered the most awkward group hug of the twentieth century.

Adalyn's parents also came forward, adding more hugs and plenty of embarrassing kisses; Mrs. Kelly went to the bathroom and had a little cry; Mr. Spencer couldn't stop smiling; and Mr. Hirtle hugged a total stranger, who just happened to walk by.

As everyone began making their way out of the education building, Adalyn announced that next year her topic would be the narwhal whales of the Arctic Ocean.

"Cool," said Henry.

Clare followed behind, feeling exceptionally proud, gleefully leaping at every morsel of fair food she could find, and thinking that this might be the best day of her whole entire life.

The End

Acknowledgments

I could say that my interest in anxiety and its impact on behavior goes back to my first year of teaching in 1973, but that's not true. That's when I first observed the connection between anxiety and behavior in a school setting. The issue of anxiety and explosive behavior actually goes back to my own childhood when I would feel physically ill if I was confronted or disciplined. Although I never exploded at school, I did at home. I remember tipping over a chest of drawers in my bedroom and screaming at the top of my lungs during an argument with my father, and I remember how my rage could overwhelm my ability to act rationally.

I first heard Temple Grandin speak in 1986 at the Autism Society of America's national conference in Detroit. Temple, an adult with autism, had just written a book about her autism entitled *Emergence: Labeled Autistic*. Temple talked about her "nerves" and the anxiety she felt in social situations. She talked about feeling overwhelmed by her senses, having explosive tantrums at school, and her intense need for relaxation.

At that same conference, I heard John McGee, co-author of *Gentle Teaching*, speak about working with aggressive children through relationship building.

These two experiences, as well as further training by Dan Hobbs, another co-author of *Gentle Teaching*, served to shape my goals, values, and beliefs as a developing teacher. I was teaching severely aggressive children with autism at the time, and I left the conference knowing that in order to solve the problems faced by my students, I had to change the way I was thinking about the behaviors I was observing. Rather than thinking that my student Mike was just "trying to get his way" or that Jane was only "trying to get attention," I would consider the role that social stress and the lack of relationship skills might play in the situation.

When creating Adalyn's fictional program in this book, I wanted to focus on the realities of social anxiety and her need to be taught relaxation strategies to combat her "nerves." I also wanted to create teachers like Miss Dudley and Mr. Spencer, who took the time to create valuing relationships with Adalyn.

Over the years, I have attended many lectures by Temple Grandin, and one thing she often says is that the primary emotion of autism is fear. As I wrote this story, that thought contributed to the creation of animal characters that could figure out Adalyn before the humans around her could. Animals seem to have fewer emotions than humans and, therefore, might have a greater understanding for the few emotions they do have. For example, fear is such a primal emotion that it made sense that Clare would be good at detecting it in Adalyn.

In 2004, I read an article from a presentation at the 7th International Conference on Human-Animal Interactions entitled "Relationships Between Young People With Autism and Their Pets" (J. McNicholas and G. M. Collis). The article suggested that pet therapy could benefit individuals with autism in learning relationship-building skills.

I started thinking seriously about investigating the use of canine therapy, and in January 2005, my husband gave me a beautiful yellow lab puppy. We named our puppy Clare after a municipal district in Nova Scotia (for real). Aside from attending obedience training with Clare, I contacted Al Peters at Can-Do-Canines (formerly Hearing and Service Dogs of Minnesota) to get the direction and training both Clare and I needed as we started our journey into the area of canine-assisted therapies and service. Although not yet trained, when she was just 3 months old, Clare began spending time with 18 children who had severe forms of autism. The objective was to desensitize her to the sounds, actions, and smells of the school. She learned to remain calm when students screamed or exhibited other aggressive behaviors.

The story line for this book was actually born when Clare attended her first session of Camp Discovery, a camp specifically developed for youth with Asperger Syndrome. Here Clare's role involved supporting highly anxious campers and campers who had a particularly difficult time making friends through a series of social routines. For example, if I observed that two campers were not getting along, I would take them on a walk with Clare. We would often play fetch with a tennis ball – Clare had learned to retrieve the ball and then return it to alternate campers. This created a social interaction routine that required subtle turn taking between the campers, often including laughter with Clare as the mediator.

The character of Adalyn is based on four different girls I have had the privilege of knowing and learning from at Camp Discovery. All four girls are highly anxious and have difficulty making friends. All four girls are brilliant academics with highly developed special interests.

In 2007, Mary Ann Messiers-Winter from the University of Oregon wrote an article entitled "From Tarantulas to Toilet Brushes: Understanding the Special Interest Areas of Children With Asperger Syndrome." In this article, Messiers-Winter discussed the social benefits of encouraging the special interests of students with Asperger Syndrome. I have always felt that relationship building between two people is primarily about mutual respect for each other's values and passions. This article solidified that idea and related it directly to autism.

As a result, the following summer, we developed special interest groups at Camp Discovery, and I was able to observe first-hand the amazing impact such groups had on relationships between campers as well as between counselors and campers. Mr. Hirtle's science club and the science room animals' ideas about finding a pack are both directly related to this experience.

Since 1991, I have done volunteer work for the Autistic Society of Trinidad and Tobago. When creating my international animal characters, it made sense to include one from my experience there. One of my favorite places to relax in the entire Caribbean is the motmot deck at The Blue Waters Inn in Speyside, Tobago, where I saw my very first motmot bird.

Many friends, family members, and colleagues have influenced my character choices. My nephew Evan has a hairless rat named Nancy, and my bonus daughter, Destiny, had a ferret named Pixie. I have a friend named Vicente and a great-nephew named Carter. My colleague Mitzi Curtis introduced me to the mantra of "I am capable," and I have a friend named Anne Dudley, who is an animal-loving teacher. Mrs. Kelly is a combination of the many excellent, innovative, and supportive special education teachers I have known.

I decided early in the process to include illustrations in the book. My nephew Lou Wisniewski had worked with me as a cartoonist on another project called *The Social Times*, a social skills magazine for children and teens ages 8-16. I approached Lou with an outline for the story and asked him if he would be interested in working on the project with me. He enthusiastically agreed to help bring my characters to life through illustration.

When I started writing my chapters, I consulted my sister-in-law, Debbie Dunn, who is a storyteller at a library in Iowa City. She made a hugely helpful suggestion: to read the story out loud as I was writing to be sure it sounded right, particularly the dialogue. Based on this advice, every day I read my latest chapters out loud to my husband, Kevin. He became my greatest cheerleader and not only listened, but also made helpful suggestions and supportive comments. Soon, I was not only having fun writing the story, I was falling in love with the characters!

I wanted to share my experiences, so I started sending chapters to family and friends, asking for their feedback. My sister, Colleen Wisniewski, became my most faithful reader. She was enthusiastic and full of praise, and on many days she kept me going by begging for the next chapter. Two other special early readers were my nephew Miles Wisniewski, Lou's brother, and my great-nephew Carter Bennett, who was 10 years old at the time.

Both during the writing phase and after I completed the first draft, many readers were willing to give me feedback. I owe tremendous thanks to my two "focus groups," 16 students and their wonderful teachers, for their generous and insightful comments about the story, the characters, and the illustrations. A big thanks goes to:

Mrs. Rosie Gavin's sixth-grade group at Nativity Grade School in St. Paul, Minnesota: Teagan Fee, Patrick Hahn, Katie Johnson, Katie Mattocks, Ethan Hennessey, Lauren Dvorak, Therese Mellum, Adriana Houge, Danny Gendreau, and Maggie Mir.

And

Mrs. Mona Watkins' third-grade group at ED Williams Elementary School in Roseville, Minnesota: Calista Loscheider, Greta Keffer, Owen Hiber, Isabella Di Nicola, Cherry Hope Jordan, and Elsa Horsted.

A very special thanks goes to my son, Colton Dunn, a comedy writer and performer; to my bonus son, Nic Buron, a freelance writer; and to my bonus daughter, Destiny Buron, a gourmet lunch truck owner and true Minnesota State Fair expert. All three took the time to read my original manuscript and give me "notes" that significantly changed how I handled some pivotal moments, such as Adalyn's ability to handle the awards ceremony at the fair.

Many others offered support, inspiration, and feedback while I was writing this book. Thank you goes to Joyce Santo, Rowan Anderson, Deb Kern, Michelle Garcia Winner, Colleen Buron, Helen Buron, Sandra Flanagan, Dr. Tony Attwood, Sarah Attwood, Tom and Mimi Fogerty, David McCoy, Gary and Joyce Hirtle, Gary, Ginny, and Millie Hirlock, Jason and Sharon Taylor, Loretta Elisworth, Dede Perkins, Sherry Auger, and everyone at the Autism Society of Minnesota.

Thank you to my father, Tom Dunn, my aunt, Patricia Hudson, and my friend Winnie Tritsch, who, with a total of 270 years among them, were my most experienced readers.

A big hug goes to my editor, Kirsten McBride, whose opinion I so admire, for responding to the story with the level of enthusiasm I had hoped for.

A special shout out goes to The Changing Tides restaurant in Bear River, Nova Scotia, where the writing began, and to Claddagh coffee shop on West 7th in St. Paul, Minnesota, where it was completed.

I must mention again my life partner, Kevin Buron, who gave me the space I needed to write, listened when I needed him to listen, and never ceased to surprise me with his clever additions to the dialogue.

Finally, thank you to my sweet and gentle Clare. I am truly inspired by your intuitive ways.